The Wrestler

The Wrestler

The Pursuit of a Dream

Bill Vincent

Table of Contents

Bill Vincent is a Christian Author and minister, who has written more than forty books to date. He now has ventured into the world of fiction to spread his wings. Whether you love this work or not, Bill is doing what he loves to do; writing, preaching and helping many to publish their very words into print. We hope you enjoy this passionate book about hopes and dreams and where one man gets the breaks to maybe see them fulfilled. Bill is the founder of Revival Waves of Glory Ministries and Revival Waves of Glory Books & Publishing.

Introduction

Nicolaus Martin has always loved wrestling. Everyone called him Nicky. As a child, he and his brothers would wrestle around as they watched the WWF, WCW and NWA. Nicky and his family were very poor. Every winter there was at least a month with no electricity at their home. No matter how poor they were, wrestling seemed to make them forget about it, even if it was only for an hour.

In the midst of everything, Nicky and his brothers had quite an imagination. They made the championship belts out of cardboard and aluminum foil. Mostly, they played around except for the few wrestling matches they had in a little town in

Illinois.

Nicky was bullied starting at the age of thirteen. The more people picked on him, the tougher he got. By age seventeen, his toughness got him noticed by a small wrestling organization. Before he knew it, he was wrestling in Japan for $50 a night. Now this was not entertainment. This stuff was real. Nicky broke his nose several times and was on the injured list more than not. He got to the point that he would not let on that he was in pain.

Nicky fought for a championship title three times and lost all three times. Two of those times were after he was sprayed in the eyes with a green mist, by the champion.

Now, Nicky was back in the States broke and broken. He heads back to the gym to see if he can resurrect those dreams of being in the big time on national television and pay per view as a professional wrestler.

Chapter One

Nicky walks in the good old gym, he grew up in. The gym itself resembles a large unemptied trash-can. The ring is extra small to assure constant battle. The lights overhead has barely enough wattage to see who is wrestling.

After Nicky gets ready, he gets in the ring. There are two heavyweights, one Caucasian the other African American. Nicky is a twenty five year old Caucasian. His face is scarred and thick around the nose. He wrestles in a slow, machinelike style. The African American wrestler dances and bangs combinations into Nicky's face with great accuracy. But the punches do not even cause Nicky to blink. He grins at his opponent and keeps grinding ahead.

The people at ringside sit on folding chairs and cry out for blood. They lean out of their seats and heckle the wrestlers. In the thick smoke, they resemble spirits. Everyone is hustling bets. The action is even heavier in the balcony. A housewife yells for somebody to cover a bet. Somebody heaves a beer can into the ring.

The African American wrestler says, "I'm gonna bust his head wide open!"

Nicky's corner man was a shriveled, balding man who is an employee of the gym is watching from Nicky's corner without any enthusiasm.

In the midst of the action, Nicky makes the sign of the cross. He was a former Catholic, but now a Christian. The wrestlers engage in battle. The other wrestler grabs Nicky in a clinch and purposely head butts him. The head butt opens a bleeding cut on the corner of Nicky's eye.

Nicky becomes furious over the hit and drives a flurry into the man's body. Nicky slams the man on the jaw and the other wrestler is out for the night. He pins him 1, 2 and 3. The fans throw garbage into the ring and Nicky ignores it.

The announcer says in a husky voice, "The winner, Nicky Martin."

Without display, Nicky climbs out of the ring and bums a cigarette from a spectator. The wrestler on the stretcher passes behind him. He watches for a moment and continues up the aisle. Before he even reaches the rear of the gym the bell rings and the next match has already begun. Nicky fades into the darkness of the rear of the gym.

Nicky has nearly completed dressing and reaches into his locker for his stuff. Also in the dingy room are a dozen other wrestlers. Two taped and ready wrestlers talk shop in the corner.

Another one paces nervously. Two other wrestlers shadowbox, while stretching and spit nervously on the floor.

The wrestler that Nicky has just defeated is drinking a beer and joking with three other wrestlers. Some of the wrestlers are smoking and the room is cloudy.

A promoter, a short man of sixty, dressed like a homeless drunk, enters. He calls out, Nicky! Nicky looks up. The promoter steps over. "Twenty five bucks for the locker an' corner man -- twelve bucks for the towel an' shower, seven for tax -- The house owes ya, fifty two fifty dollars.

The man peels off the money and departs. Nicky closes his locker, nods to the defeated wrestler, and leaves.

Chapter Two

Nicky passes a sleeping wino curled up on the sidewalk in front of a dirty grocery store. Nicky drags the man into a protective passageway.

Further down the street, Nicky pauses in front of the local bookstore. He peers into the dark store and sees a sad, huge cat sitting in the window. He mumbles to the cat and continues to the corner.

A short while later, Nicky approaches his apartment located in the most deprived section of a city in central Illinois. He kicks away the litter that has gathered against the apartment steps and enters.

The narrow hallway is painted brown. A single light bulb illuminates the gloomy passageway.

Nicky enters the one-room apartment which is drab, with a torn wrestling poster of Rick Flair and Harley Race tacked on the wall. Nailed against the far wall is a mattress. The mattress has been pounded and stuffing spills out of the center.

Nicky drops his coat on the floor, starts to boil a pan of water on his hot plate, and then flips on a cassette tape.

The tape is playing opera. As the crackling music begins, Nicky picks up his hairbrush. Using it like a microphone, he mimes to the tape. He assumes the posture of a famous singer singing to thousands of adoring fans. He then switches into a bullish wrestling stance and throws several punches. Then he does an imitation of the famous Nature Boy Rick Flair

Wooooo!

While the water boils, Nicky soaks his badly swollen hands and feet.

The next morning, Nicky passes the "bookstore". The shop is not very prosperous looking. Nicky stops at this shop every morning. He sees a girl behind the counter and presses his face against the window and makes a silly impression. The girl nervously looks away.

The girl behind the counter is Stephanie Nelson. She is not very attractive, but pleasant-looking. She is thirty five years old with light colored skin and brown hair pulled back in a ponytail. She wears glasses.

Nicky runs into his buddy, Bill.

"See the match last night?" asks Bill.

"Nah, I was in a match myself,"

answers Nicky.

"Warrior beat the bum to pieces!" Bill exclaims before Nicky turns and walks away.

Nicky makes it to Johnny's Gym. The gym is surrounded by bars. Out front is a crowd of young singers among them. Two winos lean against the entrance.

Nicky enters the gym and the place is nearly full. The sound of the beating of skipping ropes and a noisy ring of wrestlers flying around makes the room come alive, like it was a mindless piece of machinery. Over the loudspeaker music blares out. The music adds a background to the clanging.

The room is divided; fifty percent is African American, thirty percent is Latino, fifteen percent is Caucasian and five percent other nationalities.

As Nicky walks through the gym, many of the wrestlers pause to wave and yell greetings.

The dressing room is lined with dented lockers. Wooden benches, stretch across the room. Nicky goes to his locker. He tries to open it, but fails. He leans his ear against the lock and rolls the tumblers. Still, it does not open. He shakes the lock forcefully, no luck. Nicky is flustered and sits on a bench to ponder the situation.

After a moment of deep thought, Nicky stands, leaves the bench and smashes open the lock. Opening the door, he is taken back when he sees a set of very flashy clothes. "These ain't my clothes," Nicky mumbles. He sees pictures of several scantily clad African American girls taped on the inside of the door. "And these ain't my pictures."

A short, powerful man of thirty-five enters. His hair looks like it has been shaped with hedge clippers.

"Yo, Dan! What's happenin' here?"

"It ain't your locker no more," Dan quips.

"Whatta ya talkin' about it, ain't my locker no more?"

"Listen, I'm with you. But ya gotta talk to Johnny! I put ya stuff in the bag over there."

Nicky looks at his belongings crammed into a wilted shopping bag and follows Dan across the room. They move past wrestlers going through their training routines.

"See the match last night? Warrior beat that English guy bad."

"Warrior's great," replies Nicky.

Dan fakes a friendly punch at Nicky and hurries off to another chore.

The owner of the gym, Johnny, sits on a stool near the entrance. He is in his late sixties and wears a baggy sweat suit.

Nicky approaches as Johnny is conversing with another wrestler.

"I don't care what nobody says; this bum Warrior woulda never made it in the sixties!" insists Johnny.

"Hey, how ya feelin', Johnny?" asks Nicky.

"What?"

"I said, how ya feelin'?"

"Do you see me talkin'? Huh?" mumbles Johnny.

"Yeah."

"Then stand there an' wait till I'm

done. He's good, yeah, he's real fine but I gotta boy, y'know Big Crusher, who's got the stuff it takes to be a champ! He's mean, quick, an' big! What more d'ya need? Okay, go to work."

Johnny turns and looks at Nicky. "Hey! Yeah, whatta ya want?"

"I was talkin' with ya man, Dan. Hey, how come I been put out my locker?"

"Big Crusher needed it," answers Johnny nonchalantly.

Nicky turns and looks at Big Crusher warming up. Big Crusher is a young, muscular heavyweight with a mean expression.

Johnny continues, "Big Crusher's a climber! You're a banana."

"Banana?"

"Facts are facts. I run a business here.

I'm cleanin' house." Johnny pauses for a moment.

"How old are ya?"

"What?" quips Nicky.

"How old?"

"I'm twenty-three," Nicky lies.

"More like thirty," retorts Johnny.

"Twenty-three, thirty. What's the difference? It took me two months to learn the combination of that locker."

"Your body is broken down," says Johnny.

"Yeah, it's goin', that's nature. That was my locker for ten years."

"Did ya wrestle last night?" asks Johnny.

"Yeah," replies Nicky.

"Did ya win?"

"Yeah."

"Who'd ya wrestle?"

"Mike Dudley."

"Dud alright. He's a bum".

"You think everybody I wrestle is a bum."

"Ain't they?" quizzes Johnny. After a slight pause, he continues. "Ya want the truth? Ya got heart, but ya wrestle like a monkey."

"Listen, I'm gonna take a steam. I did good last night! Shoulda seen it."

"Hey, ever think about retirin'?" asks Johnny.

"No."

"Think about it."

"Yeah, sure," retorts Nicky shrugging his shoulders. And then he continues, "Shoulda seen me wrestle. I did good, y'know."

At sunset, Nicky comes down the street and pauses at the bookstore. He is eating fried chicken out of a bag. He taps on the window with a chicken bone.

Inside, Stephanie is arranging books on the counter. She hears the tapping, sees Nicky, and tenses. Nicky enters. "Good night to catch pneumonia" He states since it was ten degrees out.

Stephanie smiles slightly and moves behind the counter.

"Ah, I came in here for somethin'. Oh, yeah, would ya like somebody to walk ya home?" Nicky asks in a friendly tone.

The girl wants to say yes, but a tremendous inferiority complex will not permit it. "Sorry, not tonight. Nicky."

Nicky understands. As he exits, Stephanie watches his departure with mixed emotions.

Chapter Three

Warrior, his attorney and trainer are seated in an office of wrestling promotions. A successful promoter looks unhappy as he looks into the scowling face of Warrior.

"Are the doctor's reports confirmed?" snaps the attorney.

"Definitely," replies the promoter. Then he continues, "It says here, the number one contender has suffered a seriously cracked rib."

"Come on man," pleads Warrior.

"I suppose we could cancel the match indefinitely if you are set on wrestling him."

"It ain't just about the number one contender, what about the time

Warrior's invested," states his trainer.

"I believe we can find a solution," says the promoter.

"Solution, nothin'. What about the match?" asks Warrior.

"Don't play games with my client! Warrior has already done nearly a million dollars' worth of publicity," demands his attorney.

"A million dollars' worth!"

"And has made contractual obligations with over twenty different organizations. He doesn't want to be embarrassed," the attorney added matter of factly.

"You best find me another ranked contender an' I mean in a hurry, man!" quips Warrior.

Holding up some papers, the promoter states, "I contacted several contenders, but they are all either not ready or wrestling somewhere else."

"Then gimmie Lance Johnson. He's ranked seventh."

"He's wrestling in Japan," explains the promoter. "Why not postpone the bout until the next big event July Fourth?"

"To heck with the Fourth of July, man! Ten thousand things will be goin' down on the Fourth of July! Warrior wants to be first!" snaps the attorney.

"That may not be possible," counters the promoter.

"This man here is the star; don't cause him to get upset!" says his trainer enthusiastically.

Warrior stands beneath a poster and points to it. It just happens to be Nicolaus Martin, whom he wrestled for the championship in Japan.

"Warrior, I'm sure there's a way to salvage this," says the promoter. "I've promoted in every country in the world and I've tried to do my job to the best of my abilities. Perhaps you're right, and no one wants to be beat. I don't know what else to say."

"I do! Maybe what this match needs is something new. Now here's what's goin' down. Listen; 'cause I'm gonna say this, but one time. On February fourteenth, I'm gonna wrestle me a local poor underdog, ok? An' I'm gonna put his face on this poster with me, you hear? An' I'll tell you why, 'cause I like to give opportunity. An' all the people in the country, they'd like nothin' better than me, Warrior, to let some unknown get a shot at the greatest title in the world on this country's day of love.

Now that's the way I see it an' that's the way I want it!" says Warrior.

"It's very American," states the promoter.

"No, man, it's very smart!" quips Warrior.

Days later, back in the promoter's office, Warrior pores over a large record book. "How 'bout this Billy Knight?"

"Bum," replies the promoter.

"How 'bout this Big John?" asks Warrior.

"Too old, dull wrestler," states the trainer.

"I don't feel heat from the name," explains Warrior.

The promoter sighs. "Exactly what are you looking for, Warrior?"

"This man."

Everybody leans forward.

Warrior continues, "The Kid Nicky Martin; he's my man!"

"Nicky? His record's poor. He is not the Kid anymore."

"Don't matter! That name. It's right on," exclaims Warrior.

"He won't last fifteen minutes," says the trainer.

"Listen, I gonna carry this boy, then drop him," explains Warrior.

"I don't like you messin' with him! He can take a lot of punishment and just doesn't know when to quit. Wrestlers like that do everything wrong," replies the trainer.

"I'll drop him when I'm ready!" snaps Warrior.

While Nicky was just sitting around

with some friends, there is an argument over sports. A sport broadcast rising from the television is heard over the argument. "Unfortunate luck for Pro Wrestling #1 contender, the great former champion acquired a serious fracture of his ribs after an aggressive day of training. The champion, Warrior, says he'll be 'shopping for another victim,' to fill the vacancy for this Valentine's Day match to be held in Madison Square Garden. By the way, rumor has it that this will be the most widely-viewed sporting event in the entire world and that includes the Super Bowl, folks."

Nicky finally got the nerve to ask out Stephanie from the bookstore. After walking and talking for hours, Nicky softly kisses the woman. Her arms hang limp. He puts more passion into the kiss and she starts to respond. The passion erupts. She gives herself freely for the first time in all her years.

The following day, Nicky strolls down the street to Johnny's Gym. He climbs the stairs and enters the gym.

In a matter of seconds, his presence is known and the athletes stare in wonderment. The African American heavyweight contender, Big Crusher, throws down his towel in disgust and turns away.

Dan quietly approaches Nicky.

Hey, Nick! What happened?"

"Bout what?"

Johnny steps out of his office.

"Did ya get the message, kid?"

"What message?"

Johnny pulls out a card from his

pocket. He hands it to Nicky.

"A rep from the biggest wrestling Promotions was lookin' for ya!"

"Ya puttin' me on?" asks Nicky.

"Here's the card." replies Johnny.

"When were they here?" Nicky quizzes.

"Bout an hour ago."

"Probably lookin' for a partner for a tag team match," states Nicky.

Nicky turns from Johnny and jogs out of the gym.

"Waste of life," Johnny says from behind Nicky.

Nicky steps off a bus and hurries down the street. Every few steps he breaks into a trot.

He enters a skyscraper, exits the elevator and enters the office of Pro

Wrestling Productions.

The secretary is slightly startled by Nicky's excited expression. "May I help you?"

Nicky hands her the business card.

"Your name, please?" the secretary asks.

"Nicky. Nicky Martin"

The secretary rises and walks Nicky down the narrow hallway. She taps on the door before poking her head inside of the office. "You may go in," she announces and turns to leave.

Nicky collects himself and enters the promoter's office and eyes the multitude of sporting pictures hanging on all four walls.

The promoter warmly greets him. "Hello, Mr. Martin, I'm the Chairman of Pro Wrestling Promotions. Please, have a seat."

"Thanks," Nicky replies, his voice steady despite his nervousness.

"Mr. Martin." The promoter hesitates and begins to talk as if they are friends. "Nicky, do you have any representation? A manager?"

"No, it's just me."

"Nicky, would you be interested in..."

"Yes?"

"Excuse me."

"I know ya need partners. I'm very available," exclaims Nicky.

"I'm sure you are."

"Absolutely! Anything with the champ would be an honor."

"What?" The promoter seems very amused as he lights a cigar. "Nicky, would you be interested in wrestling

Warrior for the Championship?"

"Like I said, I'd make a great partner."

"Did you hear what I said?"

"Sure, an' I'm smart enough to know that no partner should take cheap shots at the champ. He's just there to help the man," says Nicky.

"I'm not asking you to partner with the champ. I want to know if you're interested in wrestling for the championship."

The weight of the statement comes crashing down in Nicky. For a long moment he becomes nothing more than a basket case as he ponders the statement. He half regains his senses.

"Ah...Absolutely," he says with confidence and without hesitation.

It was official. Nicky would face Warrior for the World Wrestling

Championship.

Now Nicky and Stephanie are at her home watching an old television. He smiles as the program shows Warrior being interviewed.

"How do you like the Windy City?" asks the reporter.

"I like my Chicago Brothers."

"Why did you agree to wrestle a man who has virtually no chance of winning?" asks another reporter.

"If history proves one thing, everybody gotta chance. Didn't yo' all ever hear of David an' Goliath?

"What are your feelings about the challenger?" quizzes the first reporter.

"I don't know the man."

"What does that mean?" she asks dumbfounded.

"It means if he can't wrestle, I bet he can dance!"

Nicky and Stephanie laugh at the interview.

Nicky's interview now fills the screen. Nicky squints and looks nervous under the hot lights. "This is your largest payday ever! How do you feel about it?" asks one of the reporters.

"Feel? Happy."

"How will you wrestle Warrior?"

"I'll do what I can," Nicky answers.

"Is it true the most you've ever made in a Championship match is five hundred dollars?"

"Two Fifty!" Nicky counters. "But that was a long time ago."

"And now your payday will be one hundred thousand dollars. Any comment?"

"It will be great!" Nicky replies.

They continue to watch the remainder of the interview. The head commentator is looking directly into the camera. "It's already being called by many the greatest circus in sports history. If this man lasts more than a minute I would say he's on borrowed time." He pauses as the camera zooms in. "It is matches like this with their ridiculous prices that give wrestling a bad name. Not only is this match bad; people, it is sad! Who is Nicky Martin?" he asks just before the show ends.

"Hey, I'll show them, huh, babe? It is obvious to Stephanie that the comments weigh on Nicky's mind. "I think I'm gonna train myself," he continues as he stands in her doorway. He leans in and kisses her. "See ya tomorrow."

Nicky's voice echoes in the stairwell as he moves down the stairway and continues to converse with Stephanie who remains upstairs.

Nicky heads home and Johnny meets him at his apartment. Nicky is slightly uncomfortable, almost embarrassed, at having outsiders see how he lives.

"Listen, Nick, you're a very lucky guy," Johnny says.

"Yeah," he replies.

"This is a chance of a lifetime?"

"Freak luck for sure," Nicky agrees.

"Look at all them other wrestlers. Real good boys. Good records. Colorful. Wrestle their hearts out for peanuts. But who cares? Nobody. Nobody ever gives them a shot at the title."

"Luck is a strange thing," Nicky says with an uneasy feeling.

"I'm here tellin' ya to be very smart with this shot. Like the Bible says, ya don't get no second chance."

Johnny looks hard into Nicky's eyes and continues, "Ya need a manager, an advisor. I've been in the racket fifty years. I done it all; there ain't nothin' about the world of wrestling that ain't in this head."

"Huh." Nicky lets out a loud sigh.

Johnny deafly continues, becoming more engrossed every second. "Look at this face! I had twenty stitches over the right eye, thirty over the left and my nose was busted seven times." He pauses, and then continues on. "Yeah, ya kinda remind me of me. Ya move like me. Ya got heart."

"Heart, but I ain't got anything at the gym, do I?" Nicky retorts.

I know this business, Nicky. When I was wrestling it was the dirtiest racket goin', see. Wrestlers like me were treated like dogs. They'd throw ya in the pit an' for ten bucks ya try to kill each other. We had no management." They sit in silence. "Respect, I always dished ya respect, Nicky." Johnny added.

"How can ya say that when ya gave everything to Big Crusher."

"I'm sorry, I made a mistake. Kid, I'm askin' man to man. I wanna be ya manager," Johnny pleads.

"The wrestling match is set and I don't need a manager."

"Look, you can't buy what I know. Ya can't. I've seen it all! I got pain an' I got experience."

"Whatever I got, I always got on the

shot. This shot's no different. I didn't earn nothin'; I got it on the shot. I needed ya help about ten years ago when I was startin', but ya never helped me."

"If ya wanted my help, why didn't ya just ask?"

"I did ask and you gave me nothin'," quips Nicky.

This went on for hours and finally they agreed that they needed each other. Nicky was out of shape and Johnny was up in age, so they were a perfect fit.

Chapter Four

The following morning, Nicky's alarm clock goes off at exactly five A.M. Not accustomed to rising this early, he staggers to his feet with great difficulty and wavers to the bathroom. He turns the light on and roaches scatter.

At the top of the mirror hang the telegrams he has received since he got this shot. Nicky fills the basin and submerges his face in cold water.

Nicky sways to the icebox and removes a dozen eggs. He cracks raw eggs into a glass, downs it in one swig and his body quivers. The egg drips down his chin and he wipes it off with his already stained sleeve.

Nicky steps outside dressed in a well-worn sweat suit with a hood, gloves and sneakers. It is pitch dark and his steaming breath indicates to the cold.

He begins running down the center of the deserted street. He can only be clearly seen as his form passes beneath the street lamps. Two garbage men stop heaving cans to watch him pass.

Nicky stands at the base of an overwhelmingly steep hill and stares up at it as it nearly disappears into the morning gray. Taking a deep breath, he starts up. From the start, he looks out of shape and halfway up his legs give way. Standing, he rests momentarily and descends back down the hill toward home.

Nicky passes City Hall and turns to the river. He pauses, heaving great gusts of exhausted breaths. He throws several lazy jabs in the air and walks awhile with hands on his aching sides. Men delivering the morning papers observe with amusement.

Nicky forces himself to begin running again. Heading along the street, Nicky passes beneath an elevated overpass. He is tired and slows to a jog and then begins walking again.

Later that day, Nicky goes to Johnny's gym and it is filled to capacity. The noise is deafening as Nicky pounds a heavy bag.

Johnny steps forward and removes a piece of string from his pocket. "Stop! Stop! I can't stand it! It's clumsy. You're off balance."

He motions to his brawny helper, Dan and hands him the string. "Tie it to both of his ankles and leave two feet slack."

"I never had good footwork. I'm a wrestler, not a boxer," states Nicky in his own defense.

Dan completes the task.

"Forget the footwork! You're off balance. The legs are sticking everywhere. When you can move without breakin' the string you'll have balance," explains Johnny.

"You'll be a very dangerous person," points out Dan.

Two young boys in street clothes interrupt Johnny. "Nicky, could we have your autograph?"

"Sure."

"Don't you boys ever interrupt when I'm conductin' business, or I'll kill you both! Go away!" Johnny snaps with irritation.

The boys run out.

"Autographs! Ya wanna be a writer or a wrestler? Let's work," continues Johnny.

Dan looks off across the gym.

"We got visitors."

Johnny strains his eyes to see a group of reporters and news cameramen entering his gym. "Can I help you guys?" he asks.

"Set the camera up over there, the reporter instructs to the cameraman."

"We're from channel six and we're covering the pre-match training."

"I own the place!" states Johnny.

The reporter has a hundred things on her mind. She turns from Johnny and nods to her crew as the television crew rush to set up. "Rolling here." The reporter looks into the camera. "We're here at Johnny's Gym, a landmark of sorts since 1940. The stench of toil permeates every corner. The sweat a trademark of a unique profession. Yet, the most unique fixture is an unprecedented 50 to 1 underdog heavyweight named, Nicky Martin."

The camera turns to Nicky.

"Should I do this?" he asks.

Johnny nods and Nicky faces the glaring lights. "So much has happened lately! Has it changed your lifestyle much?" the reporter asks curiosity reflecting in her eyes.

"People talk to me more," Nicky jokes.

"How are you preparing for this World Championship Match? Warrior says he'll let you stay for about fifteen minutes before he puts you away."

Nicky says with honesty, "Warrior's

a great champ."

"Do you feel you have a chance?"

"Maybe. I sure hope so!"

Nicky turns to face Johnny and he whispers in his ear. Nicky then continues, "I'll tear his head off."

"Do you have anything offensive to say about the champion?"

"Yeah, he's great," Nicky answers without knowing what the word offensive means.

Warrior and his entourage enter the gym. "I am the champion of the whole world!" he declares and everyone turns and stares in wonderment. Johnny shakes his head in disbelief. He now realizes it is a publicity stunt.

Warrior approaches Nicky. "I come to tell you to be very smart an' after this match donate what's left of your body to science!" Warrior turns to the cameras. Nicky is speechless. Warrior continues, "That's right; this match is goin' down in the history books 'cause February fourteenth I'm gonna be the first man to bounce another man out of the arena!"

Big Crusher stands in the far ring. The attention Nicky is receiving infuriates him. He slithers through the crowd like a large snake. He brushes people aside and steps behind Nicky and nudges him. Nicky thinks it is an accident and ignores it. Big Crusher pushes harder and Nicky looks questioningly at him.

"Ya nothin', Boy!"

Warrior stops his sales pitch in mid-sentence. The television crew faces Big Crusher as he continues, "I say ya nothin'!"

"What's happenin' here?" asks Johnny.

"I'm happenin'! This pig is taken' my shot! I'm a contender. He's nothin'."

Nicky is dumbstruck. "Yo', Big Crusher, why're you."

Big Crusher shakes his fist. "Wrestle me in front of these here TV reporters. I'll knock ya to the moon!"

Big Crusher's overweight, African American trainer holds up his hand and gives Big Crusher a fist bump.

"You can forget about that, kid!" quips Johnny.

"Yo' know I'm the best man here! Yo' said so yoself!"

Johnny looks apologetically to the camera crew. "Why make Nicky take a chance on cuttin' or breakin' somethin'? Take a shower, Big Crusher."

"Don't mouth me, old man, I'll knock, yo' out too. C'mon, punk, wrestle me, let everybody see who's got the heat around here."

Silence looms over the gym. Even Warrior is apprehensive as the scene becomes so real. The frightened television crew slyly begins putting away their expensive equipment.

Big Crusher continues his taunting. "Man, yo' best keep them cameras out! Wrestle me, boy! Let here see the kind of punk he's wrestling!"

Dan forces his way through the crowd and stands behind Nicky. "Don't chance it, man! He's sick."

"This is gettin' outta hand! Nicky will wrestle in the ring February fourteenth, not here!" Johnny announces matter of factly.

"Yo', old man."

"Not now, he cautions. Then Johnny goes on to explain to the crew. "See, it's very easy for a wrestler to accidentally get hurt."

Big Crusher suddenly steps forward and slaps Nicky very hard across the side of the head. The gym becomes stone cold. Big Crusher is in total command and enjoying every moment of it.

"If yo're afraid to wrestle me, then get down an' kiss my feet, boy."

Johnny looks around nervously and knows it's only seconds before the blood will run. Nicky stands motionless. Johnny says barely above a whisper, "Let's take a walk, Nick. Please, don't take a chance. He wants to hurt you so you can't wrestle."

Nicky swallows his pride. He still has the string around his ankles. He starts to shuffle away with Johnny. Big Crusher steps forward and viciously slaps Nicky again.

Dan jumps forward. "Why you tryin' to cut 'em, man! Back off, scumbag, or I'll bite your face!"

Big Crusher cuts loose with a hook and knocks Dan flat. The room reeks of fear. Warrior's eyes flick back and forth between Nicky and Big Crusher. Warrior taps his bodyguards and they begin to ease away.

"Now, boy, kiss my feet!" Big Crusher insists.

Nicky eyes his friend lying on the floor. He shuffles forward and stands before Big Crusher. Big Crusher demands, "Kiss 'em."

Nicky looks at Johnny, and then lowers his eyes to Big Crusher's feet. Big Crusher smiles. Nicky starts to bend towards the shoes. Without warning, he explodes with a pair of combinations into Big Crusher's exposed ribs. A crack is heard and Big Crusher sinks to the floor writhing in pain. The room is silent except for Big Crusher's moaning.

The gym has become a very gloomy place. Warrior is stunned by what has taken place. He eyes Nicky with admiration and a hint of apprehension and he then leaves.

Johnny is the first one to shake off the chill. He shakes his fists at the reporters, and puts his arm around Nicky. "The kid's got cannons! Print that!"

The crowd disperses, leaving Big Crusher pathetic and broken lying on a dirty gym floor.

Chapter Five

They enter the depressing apartment. On the floor are at least ten telegrams. Nicky scoops them up and tosses them aside. Next to the door is a pile of over a hundred telegrams.

"Don't you open them anymore?" quips Stephanie.

"They either say, 'Kill the champ' or 'Hope you die.' What ya got in the bag?" Nicky asks, changing the subject.

Stephanie steps to the window and pulls some lovely curtains from a shopping bag. The colorful curtains brighten the otherwise dark room. "Do ya like 'em?"

"Sharp. They're real nice."

"Really? You don't think they're

overly feminine?"

"No, they're sharp. And you look great!"

Stephanie smiles and pulls out a small wreath. Nicky smiles. His eyes show what he feels for this woman.

"Stephanie, you really look great, but y'know I can't fool around durin' trainin'. It makes the legs weak."

"Don't want weak legs," she teases him.

"Yeah, but weak legs ain't bad sometimes, y'know," he replies with a wink.

Nicky approaches in a seductive manner. Stephanie uncharacteristically removes her sweater. Underneath is a T-shirt that reads, "Go Nicky."

"I thought it might be cute."

"Ya right." Nicky laughs. "Maybe we best just hold hands. The shirt made me feel guilty, y'know."

Later, Nicky left to work out. He built what looked like a children's playground. There were monkey bars and he would make up his own obstacle course. Nicky would swing from the monkey bars while doing pull ups on every bar, then run through several tunnels. At the end, he would pick up two bales of hay and slam them on the ground. It was a sight to see, but it was making him stronger and faster.

Meanwhile, Johnny is in his cluttered, dark office above the gym. Blankets are tacked over the windows. After his workout, Nicky joins him to watch videos of Warrior in action. Nicky watches the video with intense concentration as the wrestler moves around the ring like a huge dancer.

"His defense is great; can't lie 'bout that! You have a rollin' style. Can't retreat as fast. But your style ain't retreatin'," says Johnny.

They both watch the flickering images. "See how he plays sometimes. Nobody knows his next move, him included," adds Johnny.

They watch more action. Warrior has a wrestler helpless against the ropes. "Killer instinct! Ya both got the killer touch. Interestin'. See that! Right-cross combination. Beautiful. But you got the power to rip the body. We will have to use your punching power," explains Johnny.

They watch more action and Johnny continues rambling on. "Nicky, when ya climb into the square, an' know ya' meetin' the best wrestler in the world, ya' gonna be ready, ya' gonna be ready 'cause I been waitin' for too many years. When I'm done with you, you'll gonna be able to sleep on nails. "You'll be a very, very dangerous person. " He pauses briefly. "We are going to have to get you some finishing moves. You need at least two or three. We ought to get you a submission move to. All great wrestlers learn their opponents finishing move. I think it will be best to be ready for anything."

After watching the videos, Nicky pounds the heavy bag with intense concentration. As he strikes from all angles, Johnny instructs.

Nicky now works on the incline sit-up board, while doing sit-ups; he pounds himself in the stomach with a dumbbell. The pain is evident on his face.

Then he does pushups between two chairs as Dan sits on his shoulders. Johnny's coaching drives him on.

Nicky learns how to use the ropes like a cruiser weight. He flies through the ropes like a trapeze artist.

Dan has on a pair of target gloves and Nicky moves around the ring swinging at them. Nicky is working on a knockout blow. He is attempting to run and hit his target with a round punch. By the 20th swing, he hits it on even knocks Dan through the ropes.

"We will call that 'The Knockout Punch!'" exclaims Johnny.

Nicky worked slamming the two bales of hay to the mat. He would heave them over his head and slam them down.

"We will call that your 'Power Bomb'. We will also make your submission move the cross-face," states Johnny.

Drenched in sweat, Nicky rolls in and out of the ring with speed. His expression is hard and flushed. Johnny clicks a stopwatch and pats Nicky's shoulder. He is very happy.

Nicky has just completed exercising with the medicine ball. Dan hands him a towel.

Nicky now has enough energy left to go for a run. Dashing through the streets, he resembles a cheetah.

It is evening and Nicky is alone at the very bottom of a huge hill that seems to stretch into the heavens. This is the same hill that he couldn't even make it to the top of before. Nicky takes a deep breath and sprints up the never-ending hill. Halfway up, his body shows the strain. Nearing the top, he pumps with all his strength and arrives at the very top. He looks down the steep hill and swells with pride. He is ready.

Chapter Six

Nicky is led into the Mayor's office by an assistant. Nicky is very nervous as he approaches the mayor, who is seated behind his wide desk. "Sit down, Nicky." He flips open a thick file that lies in front of him. Then he continues. "I've been going over your record. You've been busy over the years...expelled from school for fighting, nine arrests -- probation."

Nicky tries to sink into the chair.

The mayor continues on. "I'm a very busy man, but I just wanted to remind you that you'll be setting an example for thousands of guys like yourself and maybe start them off in a new direction and give our police force a break. I also hope you try your very best and bring pride to this city."

"Yes Sir. I'll try my best," replies Nicky.

The mayor presses a button and a photographer enters.

"Would you stand up, please?" the mayor asks cordially.

Nicky rises and the mayor shakes his strong hand. Their picture is taken three times and then the photographer exits.

"Thank you for coming by, Nicky. Good luck."

"Any time," says Nicky.

The mayor sits back down. "Wait...After the wrestling match you'll have nearly a hundred thousand dollars. What do you plan to do with it?"

Nicky smiles, and then answers,

"Run for mayor."

The mayor is shocked at first, but then breaks into a big, friendly laugh and Nicky exits.

Stephanie and Nicky are at his apartment looking at Newsweek Magazine. The headline reads: "Nicky Stands with Mayor."

"Nicky, do you realize everybody in this country knows your face, and after yah' wrestle everybody in the world is going to."

"Yeah..." was all he could muster. It seems too good to be true.

The telephone rings and Nicky rises and walks to the new white object hanging on the wall. He never had a phone in his home before now. He covers the receiver with his hand. "My first call," he whispers to Stephanie.

"Hello? Yeah, Nicky speakin'. Who is this? Brad? Brad, who? Oh, hey Brad! How ya been? I ain't seen ya for eight or nine years. Yeah, things are great! How's things with you upstate? Ya sellin' real estate, hey, that's a good job. Yeah, I gotta advance, but I bought ringside seats for the guys at the gym. I get the hundred grand after the match."

Stephanie overhears the statement.

"Yeah, I know it's a lotta money! Condominiums? Everybody uses them. Listen, I think a pet shop is a good investment, y'know. I don't care 'bout long hours…there's no depreciation…that don't matter none to me. Yeah, I like animals. Why don't ya give me ya number an' I'll call ya back? Let me getta pencil." Nicky makes no effort to get a pencil. "Okay, what is it. Yeah, yeah, thanks for callin'. Sure I'll get back to ya, Brad see ya." Then Nicky hangs up.

"What was that you said about a pet shop?"

Nicky seems distant. "What?"

"What did you say about a pet shop?"

"I don't want ya workin' for nobody else no more."

"Is everything all right?" asks Stephanie with concern.

"I gotta go out for a while. I just want to take care of ya." Nicky replies then grabs his coat and moves to the front door.

He arrives at Johnny's Gym and unlocks the door. He moves through the eerie shadows of the gym and up the steps to Johnny's office. At the top of the stairs, he looks down at the ring, reflects for a moment, and then enters the office.

After turning on the lights, he quickly cleans the cluttered desk and sets up the video. He goes to the cabinet and removes a stack of videos.

The office clock indicates it is several hours later. Nicky is engrossed in watching another Warrior video. He sits motionless and something catches his eye. He stops the video as Warrior is delivering his finishing move to an unfortunate opponent. Nicky moves right up to freeze frame and inspects it like it was a priceless painting. He backs off and begins writing on a note pad.

The first light of dawn streams through Johnny's filthy windows. Nicky is slumped in a chair and it is apparent he has lost interest in watching the videos.

The door opens and Johnny flips on the light. Nicky rubs his reddened eyes. The two men stare at each other for a long moment. Johnny studies Nicky's despondent expression and knows what is on the wrestlers mind.

"I know what you're thinkin' kid. At least ya gotta shot. All ya can do is try ya' best!" says Johnny.

Nicky stands and, inches past Johnny and exits the room. Johnny walks over and turns off the video. He idly pushes the machine with a lazy motion until it slides off the desk and crashes to the floor.

After leaving Johnny's gym, Nicky listlessly moves down the street and heads for home. When he arrives at his apartment, Stephanie is asleep on the couch. He lowers himself beside her. Her eyes open.

"I can't do it."

"What are you talking about?" asks Stephanie.

"I can't beat him."

"Warrior?" she quips.

"Yeah, I can't beat him."

Stephanie touches his face.

"I been watchin' the videos and studyin'. He ain't weak nowhere."

"What're we going to do?"

"I don't know."

"Oh, Nicky, you worked so hard," says Stephanie.

"It ain't so bad, 'cause I was a nobody before."

"Don't say that!" she exclaims.

"C'mon, it's true! But that don't bother me. I just wanna prove somethin'! I ain't a bum. It doesn't matter if I lose. Don't matter if he opens my head. The only thing I wanna do is go the distance! That's all. Nobody's ever gone with this guy. If I go and I'm still standin', I'm gonna know then I'm not just another bum from the neighborhood.

Stephanie touches Nicky's face. The wrestler gently lowers himself beside his woman. "What about a last man standing match? You won't stay down. You said it yourself."

Nicky calls Johnny to make it happen.

Chapter Seven

It is the night of the match at Madison Square Gardens and the arena is filling to capacity. Grandly dressed celebrities and wealthy wrestling fans lower themselves into their ringside seats. Nearly everyone is in the colors of the champ, which are red, white and blue.

The arena is decorated with tons of patriotic red, white and blue. High above the ring are huge posters of Nicky and Warrior.

Warrior sits in his dressing room. It is dead silent except for some noise from the arena that filters under the door. The rasping sound of the adhesive tape is very pronounced as Warrior's hand is being taped.

Warrior is ready for a fight, not a

wrestling match. It's a last man standing match. You must knock your opponent down and out so he doesn't get back to his feet by the count of ten.

Dead silence except for the sound of the tape and Warrior's breathing as his other hand is being wrapped.

The atmosphere in Nicky's dressing room is identical to that in Warrior's dressing room. Stephanie watches in silence as Dan wraps Nicky's hand. Again, the most pronounced sound is the rasping of the adhesive tape and his mounting breathing pattern as Nicky's other hand is being wrapped.

Some drops are placed in Nicky's nose. A heavy coating of Vaseline is applied around Nicky's eyes. In an extreme close-up, several deep scars are visible.

Everyone present in the dressing room is motionless as Nicky exits the room. Alone, in the bathroom, Nicky is on his knees praying. Completing his silent prayer, he stands and looks at himself in the mirror. Suddenly a wave of emotion sweeps over him as he thinks that in a few moments he will face the most overwhelming challenge of his life.

Back in the dressing room, the door opens and a security guard leans in and nods that it is time. After he leaves, Nicky steps out.

"It's time, kid!" announces Johnny.

Nicky nods and moves toward Stephanie.

"I'll wait for you here," she says on the verge of tears.

Nicky nods and she kisses him. Then

Nicky, Johnny and Dan start down the long hallway. Up ahead are three security guards. Nicky rubs his bare shoulders then puts on the robe with his name embroidered across the back.

There are two ringside commentators sitting in front of a panel of closed circuit televisions. "We would like to welcome our viewing audience to Madison Square Garden's main event for the World Championship Match; the first major event of the Year. A point of interest is that the match is being beamed to more than seven hundred and fifty million fans in theatres in nearly every corner of the world. I would like to welcome an old friend, and co-commentator for this evening's event, Todd White."

"Thank you, Jim. The electricity is everywhere tonight. Nicky Martin, a fifty-to-one underdog, is living a Cinderella story which has captured peoples' imaginations all over the world. From the increase in sound of the crowd it appears the challenger is now approaching the ring. His record is forty-six wins, twenty four losses."

"I only wonder if this man has the skill to go past three minutes. The odds say, 'No,'" remarks the first commentator, Jim.

Nicky comes down the ramp and there is a lot of mixed emotions. Some are shouting, "Nicky! Nicky! Nicky!" and others are chanting, "You suck!"

The champion enters and wow, what a combustible sound of enthusiasm.

"You could go deaf with the noise! It undoubtedly means the champion, Warrior, is heading towards the ring," says the second commentator, Todd.

"I want you! I want you!" he exclaims to Nicky as he enters the ring. The crowd loves the taunting. Warrior floats back to his corner.

"Don't let 'em get you tight," says Johnny.

"Whatta ya think his outfit cost?" asks Nicky.

The Announcer steps to the center of the ring. "Ladies and gentlemen, welcome to Madison Square Garden's World Championship Match! We are very proud to have with us sixteen times World Champion, Rick Flair."

Rick Flair waves to the crowd and greets both wrestlers.

The announcer points and the timekeeper rings the bell. "Now it's time for the evening's main event! In the corner to my right, the challenger, at one hundred an' ninety-five pounds, Nicky Martin!" yells the announcer, his voice deep and precise.

There is a good response from the crowd.

"In the far corner, weighing in at two hundred and ten pounds, The Undisputed Champion of the World, 'The Louisville Slugger' Warrior! boasts the announcer in a deep baritone.

The arena explodes with applause and he puts on a display of hand speed.

The referee motions to both wrestlers. They step to the center of the ring. As the referee explains the rules Warrior and Nicky stare hard into each other's eyes. The referee's voice fades and the wrestlers' expressions fill the ring. Something soulful and frightening is being communicated.

"Now come out wrestling," instructs the referee.

The Wrestlers return to their corners.

"God bless ya, Nick," says Johnny.

"Thanks, Johnny. I'm gonna try," Nicky replies.

Chapter Eight

The bell rings and the champ dances forward and boxes Nicky as though he considers the man an amateur.

"The champ stings the slower challenger with jabs at will. Martin blocks eighty percent of the blows with his face and doesn't look the best he's ever been but is moving smoothly. He snaps out a triple combination that backs Martin into a corner and he then monkey flips Martin to the mat," explains the commentator.

"The champion is smiling and toying with the man! He's trying to give the fans their money's worth and make a show of it. Another left to right combination. The champ does his finishing move, the pedigree" says the second commentator.

"Martin is down!" exclaims the commentator.

"At the count of only five, Nicky suddenly explodes with an upswing hook to the jaw and the champ is dropped. The arena explodes and the spectator's eyes show disbelief. So does Nicky's."

Nicky backs into his corner. "You can do it! You got the power! Get the body, get the body! Ya got him goin'!" yells Johnny.

"Six! Seven! Eight!" counts the referee.

"He is up. His playful attitude is gone and he is now all business. His lightning jab stings Nicky's face repeatedly," says one of the commentators.

"Come at me, sucker!" taunts Warrior.

Nicky charges and a terrific right jab crashes against Warrior's chin, followed by an uppercut to the liver that causes the champ to cringe. Nicky bounces the champ off the ropes into a power bomb. Nicky is too impassionate to leave the champ down for the count.

Warrior counters with jabs and Nicky whips brutal combinations to the body.

Nicky rushes out fast and furious. Warrior melts out a left hook that raises a goose egg over Nicky's eye. Warrior employs footwork that dazzles Nicky. He has class. He studies Nicky and employs his lightning jab with cutting accuracy. Still Nicky shuffles ahead, bombarding his midsection with hooks. The champ throws Nicky around like a bag of potatoes.

It nearly ends when Warrior assaults Nicky with blinding combinations and then delivers a stupendous right cross close line that flings Nicky into the ropes and shatters his nose.

Warrior stands in his corner and jokes with the fans, but he is beginning to show the strain from the body punches.

"Man, I rearranged his face with that right! The people love what's happenin' tonight!" brags Warrior.

The medical staff checks Nicky's nose and sure enough it is broke. They try to cancel the match, but Nicky just says, "No, I'm wrestling'"

The commentators are caught up in the action. They speak rapidly into their microphones. "If you had asked anyone who knows wrestling, they never would've predicted this. Nicky has a chance, explains one of the commentators.

"Warrior comes out dancing. He skips and sidesteps Nicky's sledge hammer hook. An expert ring general, Warrior uses the ring fully. Nicky keeps tearing in and meets the bombing attack that causes thick swelling. Nicky fires a penetrating punch to the heart," says the commentator as he describes the action. After a brief pause, he continues on. "Warrior almost sprints out of the corner, feints and throws a pair of left-right combinations. Martin drops beneath a left uppercut and lands a very solid shot on his temple -- not much movement from Martin, duck a left, a right, another left and explodes with a right hook to the temple. The champ backs off," says the commentator as he gives a play by play of the action.

"There's no way Warrior expected this kind of hitting power!" exclaims the second commentator.

"The brilliant ability of the Champion to master situations like this is one of his most outstanding traits! He tosses a perfect right hand that strikes Nicky," announces the commentator.

"On the offensive, Martin takes the punishment and counters with a left flush over the heart. Oh, that had to hurt!" counters the second commentator before he continues. "The wallop knocks Warrior off balance. Nicky releases a terrifying uppercut that opens a gash under his eye, and his face contorts with excruciation."

"Nicky follows with a close line."

"That man's takin' his job too serious," says Warrior as he stares at Nicky.

"Nicky's face is in very bad shape, not cut, but wretchedly swollen around the eyes," announces the commentator.

Meanwhile, Stephanie is unable to remain alone. She is lured by the growing roar of the fans. She exits the dressing room and walks down the corridor. The increasing cheers make her speed up. She opens the door at the end of the corridor and is hit by a thunderous wave of sound. The guard at the door inspects her and goes back to watching the match. Stephanie stands at the rear of the arena and watches the battle. She is engrossed by the power of it all.

Back in the ring, Nicky keeps grinding ahead. He plants a thumping left over the champion's heart and gasps. Nicky is game but losing.

The men are wrestling with appalling tenacity. Nicky rips and tears into the body. Warrior counters with a ceaseless stream of windmill like lefts. The challenger is seriously outclassed.

Nicky wades in and employs incredible footwork. The champ sets himself and cuts loose with a thunderbolt right cross to Nicky's already broken nose. Blood sprays from the wound and red droplets drip from his chin.

Nicky takes a merciless beating and is staggered by a torrent of combinations. Nicky's eyes are closed, but the champ cannot drop him.

The commentators shift in their seats. "Without a doubt this is the most punishing brawl I have ever seen! The ringside audience is spotted with blood. The champ has never been pushed to this limit," exclaims one of the commentators. After a brief pause, he continues. "This match should have been stopped long ago, but Nicky Martin refuses to fall."

"Not only has he refused to fall, but he has beaten the champion's body without mercy and the match has become a vicious slugfest," remarks the second commentator.

Johnny yells, "Wanna keep goin'?" at Nicky.

"Would you keep goin'?" Nicky counters.

"Yeah," he replies.

At the rear of the arena, Stephanie looks transfixed at the ring. She is caught up in the heat of the battle. Then she takes a moment to bow her head and pray.

Nicky bores in close, but Warrior still has spring in his legs. He seems determined to end it this round. Warrior catches Nicky flush on the jaw causing him to stagger. Like a beast, Warrior cuts loose with pure savagery. Nicky is driven against the ropes and receives a devastating beating from the champion. Nicky is dropped. The champion picks up Nicky and gives him yet another finishing move, the pedigree and then gives him another one. That is two pedigrees in a row.

Nicky lies stunned in the middle of the ring. Everything seems distorted as he looks for familiar faces. Johnny screams frantically for him to stay down.

"Six, seven, eight," continues the referee.

Nicky gets to his feet and tenses with renewed energy. He is like a wounded wild animal. The tide suddenly turns. Nicky drops down low and catches Warrior with a pair of terrific body punches that seem to drive Warrior's diaphragm up to his throat. A glaze of pain covers Warrior's eyes. It is only with supreme effort that keeps the Champion upright. Warrior is badly hurt. He is bent over.

Nicky moves towards Warrior. Warrior flicks dread jabs into Nicky's eyes. Nicky wades in with punches that seem to cause Warrior's back to take the punishment. Nicky gives the champ yet another Power Bomb and then puts a Cross-Face submission move on. It's a Last Man Standing Match, even if the champ taps out it won't be over until a ten count. The champ is tapping, but the bell won't ring. Nicky releases the hold.

From his knees, Warrior leans over Nicky and blood drips from his mouth down on Nicky's neck and shoulders, as the champ climbs up Nicky's warn body.

"I think my ribs are broken," spats Warrior to his manager.

Blood trickles from the corner of Warrior's mouth. The trainer feels the ribs. "You're bleedin' inside, man?" quizzes the trainer.

"Don't stop anything. This guy was a nobody. I have to finish it," says the Warrior.

"Don't kill yourself, man. Cover the ribs! Look here, elbow down, tight and stand straight. You're the best, you're the best!" encourages his trainer.

Nicky no longer resembles himself. His face has completely been beaten to jelly, but his mood is buoyant. He is approaching the supreme moment of his life. He cannot be bothered with pain or doctors.

Everyone is distraught over Nicky's dangerous condition but Nicky and Warrior are back in middle of the ring. Warrior moves cautiously out of his corner and circles to Nicky's right.

The commentators stare in awe at the wrestlers. This stuff is for real. It's not about entertainment any more. It is about the World Wrestling Championship.

"The wrestling has slowed down to a near stand-still. The champ circles to

Nicky's right. The spectrum is nearly silent. Neither wrestler has made a motion to throw. I've never seen anything like it in sixty three minutes of a championship match. Warrior spits blood on the canvas. It appears he is protecting his right side. His ribs were probably injured," says the commentator. He pauses briefly and then continues. "It's confirmed, unofficially, his ribs may be broken. Warrior fakes a left and throws a big tired right. Martin attacks with one hand!"

Warrior throws a fake punch and Nicky falls for it. The Champion unleashes a lethal blow to the side of the head that jolts Nicky into the first row. Nicky sags on the barricade in a crucified position. The insane crowd leaps to their feet.

Nicky's bloody teeth snarl at Warrior and he waves him to come ahead and wrestle toe to toe. Warrior obliges with a weary but an effective burst of rights and lefts that have knock out written on every punch. Nicky counters the assault blow for blow.

Blood sprays over the ropes and onto the ringside photographers. They are horrified and wipe away the blood.

The wrestlers stand toe to toe and drag every remaining bit of strength from their souls and beat each other without mercy. They look like they are in a trance and have entered a dimension far beyond blood and pain.

As the champ swings a hefty right hook, Nicky moves and catches the champion in his own finishing move.

The referee is exhausted and the

count is long and slow. "One…two…three…four," counts the referee as Nicky is leaning on the ropes. "Five…six…" the referee continues as the champ reaches for the ropes. "Seven…eight…nine," and the champ falls from his knees to the mat. "Ten!" exclaims the referee. The bell rings and the arena explodes with thunderous approval.

The managers rush to their collapsed wrestlers. In the midst of all the confusion, both wrestlers look at each other with blatant respect. They stand like blood-drenched gladiators on the most dramatic night of their lives.

As though reacting to some unspoken command, they both step towards each other and embrace. Warrior whispers into Nicky's ear. "Welcome to the big leagues, Son."

Johnny comes over and separates them and leads Nicky to his corner and then Johnny embraces him.

The Announcer enters the ring with a microphone. "Attention, please! Attention! Ladies and gentlemen, tonight we have had the rare privilege to have witnessed the greatest exhibitions of stamina and guts ever in the history of all of sports," exclaims the announcer, his voice raspy with excitement.

The crowd roars. "Ladies and gentlemen, The Winner and New World Wrestling Champion Nicky Martin!" shouts the announcer.

Nicky sorely smiles and looks at the waves of cheering fans that circle the ring and reach out towards him. Johnny grabs Nicky's hand and raises it.

The crowd roars even louder.

Johnny and Nicky look at each other and grin. Johnny hugs Nicky like a son and raises Nicky's hand again. Nicky stares across the ring at Warrior. The two men lock stares that reflect admiration.

Warrior climbs out of the ring and the fans crush forward screaming his name and waving red, white and blue banners.

Nicky also climbs out of the ring and waves of frantic, well-wishing fans rumble forward. Johnny's eyes show mounting apprehension as the fans become abnormally active.

Nicky and Warrior's fans are aggressively competing against each other. Nicky's fans counter by bellowing, 'Nicky! Nicky! Nicky!'

Finally, Stephanie presses through the crowd. "I love you, I love you, I love you..." she repeats to Nicky. The two are swept along into the greatest night anyone can remember.

"Stephanie, will you marry me?"

The crowd was too loud for him to even hear her answer.

Later, the chairman of World Wrestling Federation finds Nicky at the hospital.

"What a match Nick! You Mind if I call you Nick?"

"No, it's fine."

The chairman asks, "Will you give Warrior a rematch?"

"Not tonight," replies Nicky.

"I want to personally offer you a contract with us after you heal up. You have the heart that is rare to see. If you will accept our offer, I would want you to make an appearance on our Monday Night Show.

"What do you think?" asks Nicky.

Stephanie replies, "I think it would be a great opportunity. Is that what you want?"

Nicky says to the chairman, "Well...."

THE END

The questions remain. Will there be a rematch? Will Nicky be at the next Monday Night Show? Will Stephanie and Nicky get married? Will Nicky accept the contract offer?

Recommended Books

By Bill Vincent

Overcoming Obstacles
Glory: Pursuing God's Presence
Defeating the Demonic Realm
Increasing Your Prophetic Gift
Increasing Your Anointing
Keys to Receiving Your Miracle
The Supernatural Realm
Waves of Revival
Increase of Revelation and Restoration
The Resurrection Power of God
Discerning Your Call of God
Apostolic Breakthrough
Glory: Increasing God's Presence
Love is Waiting – Don't Let Love Pass You By
The Healing Power of God
Glory: Expanding God's Presence
Receiving Personal Prophecy
Signs and Wonders
Signs and Wonders Revelations
Children Stories
The Rapture
The Secret Place of God's Power
Building a Prototype Church
Breakthrough of Spiritual Strongholds
Glory: Revival Presence of God
Overcoming the Power of Lust
Glory: Kingdom Presence of God
Transitioning to the Prototype Church
The Stronghold of Jezebel
Healing After Divorce

A Closer Relationship With God
Cover Up and Save Yourself
Desperate for God's Presence
The War for Spiritual Battles
Spiritual Leadership
Global Warning
Millions of Churches
Destroying the Jezebel Spirit
Awakening of Miracles
Deception and Consequences Revealed
Are You a Follower of Christ
Don't Let the Enemy Steal from You!
A Godly Shaking
The Unsearchable Riches of Christ
Heaven's Court System
Satan's Open Doors
Armed for Battle
The Wrestler
Spiritual Warfare: Complete Collection
Growing In the Prophetic
The Prototype Church: Complete Edition
Faith
The Angry Fighter's Story

To Order:

Email:
rwgcontact@yahoo.com

Web Site:
www.revivalwavesofgloryministries.com

Mail Order:

Revival Waves of Glory
PO Box 596
Litchfield, IL 62056

Shipping $5.00
If you mail an order and pay by check, make check out
to Revival Waves of Glory.

Most books are in multiple formats such as Hardcover,
Soft-Cover, Ebook (such as Kindle & Nook), and Audio
Books.